KARMA

by

Mary Boyle

Margaret Regan

Two of the Regan sisters

Dedications

This book is dedicated to all the people who have lost their homes, pensions, school funds and anyone else who has lost substantial savings due to the economic meltdown of 2008.

Table of Contents

Prologue

KARMA was written to enlighten the populace as to the reasons behind the economic meltdown of 2008. The story seeks to entertain while imparting the financial information so the reader will not have to prop their eyelids open with toothpicks.

KARMA is a light drama centered around an Irish Catholic family whose teenage son Patrick went to prison for blowing up a bank fifteen years ago. Now he's getting out of prison a reformed man, but seeing the banking mess, he sets out for revenge.

Nick, his cousin and main character, has a respectable government job but is an emotional cripple, racked with guilt due to the fact that his cousin went to prison and took the rap for both of them.

Nick and a beautiful young Mexican hacker build a super computer based on quantum physics and PlayStations® incorporating fiber optics.

Using their super computer, they hack into the Federal Reserve Bank and all of the secret accounts of the major players in the bank debacle. As they set things right according to ninety-nine percent of the population, they must avoid going back to jail for illegal hacking.

Any similarity to any of the names in the book is purely coincidental.

Chapter One Wake up Nick

In Nick's dream he sees a big explosion. Two boys are running. Nick as a fifteen year old cannot pick up his legs to run. Heavy, so heavy, then a hand clamps down on him.

Nick awakens with a jolt. His room is a sparsely furnished bedroom. A bed, chest of drawers, only blinds on the windows, a plain brown bedspread and worn blue pillow cases. He is perspiring and frightened.

His bedmate, Alice awakens. She says, "Bad dream?"

Nick replies, "It's nothing, go back to sleep." He gets up to get some H2O and takes his phone with him to the kitchen. It's 12:10 AM. Nick thinks to himself, *Too late to call Uncle John*.

Alice mutters to herself, "I am going back to sleep. I have to work in the morning." Nick goes back to bed, covers himself, but lies with eyes open.

A little while later, Nick slowly get up for work. He shuffles to the bathroom with its peeling old wallpaper inside. Nick sadly looks into the mirror and realizes he looks much older than he should. Fifteen years of nightmares and guilt will do this. Maybe he'll feel better when Pat gets out. He thinks of getting some makeup from Alice's purse, then thinks the better of it. Better to wear the martyrdom and guilt like a badge.

Distracting himself, he starts to shave and shower, then departs for work.

Karma

Chapter Two Another Day at Work

The next morning, Nick is riding the "L" train and passes through shabby neighborhoods with worn-out clothes hanging on sagging laundry lines. It then plunges into darkness as it descends into the subway. Nick exits the train and ascends stairs that lead to the pace of the perpetually preoccupied. This against the background of the man-made God's country that is downtown Chicago.

He takes out his phone and punches in a number.

"Hey Uncle, what ya doin' today?" says Nick.

"Nothing. I'm retired," quips Uncle John.

"How about we meet for lunch? Patrick gets out next week," says Nick.

Uncle John replies, "I know. You're gonna come with me downstate to get him aren't you?"

"You bet! Lunch?" proposes Nick.

Uncle John comes back with, "You buying?"

"Sure," Nick says.

"Meet you at The Palm at noon" pipes Uncle John.

Nick rolls his eyes, *Always the most expensive for Uncle John*, he thought to himself.

"Noon then," Nick comes back with.

Nick walks into his work building on LaSalle and rides to the 22nd floor and into the office where the sign over the door says "Information Specialist - USA". He walks past the plump secretary, Tess, sitting in front of his office with his name "Nick Cusack" on the door. Alan, his boss, calls him to come to his office. Alan has an untidy appearance and wears a very bad

Karma

toupee. This is topped off by an abrasive personality..

"Hey Nick. Where's that report? I'm late for my meeting?" Alan delivers in a short manner.

Nick, trying to wipe the disgusted look off his face, "Right here, boss."

"It doesn't have too many of those technical words does it? I want everyone to understand it," demanded Alan.

Nick, under his breath, "Don't you mean so you can understand?" He then replies audibly, "Yes, Alan, it should be perfectly clear."

"You're dismissed," quips Alan.

Chapter Three Nick Reminisces

Nick, now back in his office, pulls up on his computer a twenty-year-old story of a bank branch explosion. Next to the story is a picture of a fifteen-year-old Patrick who was charged with the crime. Nick flashes back to a courtroom scene. A reporter outside is reporting the story of Patrick's conviction.

Reporter states, "Police found a glove fifty yards from the explosion with Patrick's name neatly printed inside." His mother had always written his name in his gloves as he had a habit of leaving them at school. Patrick admitted his involvement to police after 6 hours of interrogation. He explained how he got the explosives and why. He was angry. The bank had foreclosed on their family home after his father's tragic untimely death. His mother was only one payment behind on their mortgage, and he wanted revenge. He insisted he had acted alone. He pleaded guilty and received a fifteen-year sentence as the court decided to treat him as an adult.

Nick thought back to that day. In Nick's mind's eye, there was a huge explosion! It was the bank building that blew up and burned, lighting the night sky. The building was surrounded mostly by parking lot and two fifteen-year-old boys were running from the blast.

Nick screams, "Run! Run!"

Patrick screams back, "What's it look like I'm doing? I'm running out of breath!"

They stop at a safe distance to survey their handiwork – jumping, high fives – laughing and doubling over as they jog home.

The houses lining the street are brick bungalows with a few wood-sided houses. Well-tended landscaping aside, lots are neglected with weeds and dead grass. Cars parked on the street, midsized, some clean, some rusted. Street is tree lined, but no leaves as fall has felled them.

Karma

Nick states, "Did you ever think that since our mothers are identical twins we are more like brothers than cousins?"

Patrick replies, "How so?"

Nick elaborates, "Because they are identical, that means they are genetically the same, so it's like we have the same mother genetically."

Patrick comes right back, "Cool! I never did think of that."

Long pause as they are still jogging home.

Patrick continues, "Yeah, but they are REALLY different!"

Nick, "Yeah, they sure are."

They reach an old bungalow with tended landscape, carefully planted shrubs in front, decorative rocks on side of house (gangway). They jog to back of the house, up stairs to the porch, open back door. Bright kitchen light floods out as they enter the house.

Nick's mother, Joan, is standing in kitchen. At the sight of the boys, she puts her hands on her hips and adopts the interrogation look that all mothers of teenagers have learned to display.

Joan pipes, "Where have you two been?"

Patrick, "Just out having a blast."

Nick covers his face to hide the laugh.

Joan cries, "Well, you missed dinner, and I'm not reheating it so do it yourself!"

Patrick's mother, Jean, is standing at stove. She is the identical twin of Joan but looks remarkably unlike Joan. She wears a nervous look and the cowed posture of a spirit that has been broken.

Jean says, "I'll do it, and I'll clean up too."

Joan and Nick walk out of kitchen leaving Pat and his mother alone.

Patrick says sullenly, "Do you miss our old life—before Dad died and when we had our own house? Before the bank took it?"

Jean replies, "It's no good to dwell on it now."

Patrick quickly replies, "That's what Aunt Joan says isn't it?"

Jean says, "And she's right. After all, you can't change things now. We all need to move forward."

Patrick turns to walk away while mumbling, "A little revenge can help ya move on."

Jean appears to have not heard.

Nick and Pat get ready for bed. After the boys are sent to bed, they are awake and can hear conversation between their mothers.

Joan moans, "Honestly, Jean, since I took you in, I feel the boys are getting out of control! I discipline Nick and he listens, but you let Patrick get away with murder. Where's your backbone?"

Jean says, "I'm sorry, Joan, and I really appreciate you taking us in, but he just lost his father."

Joan throws back the ball, "That was a year ago; you have to put the fear of God in him, Jean, or you're going to lose him too! I just know they were up to no-good tonight. (Softly) You're my sister and I love you, and I love to help you out, but God, Jean, I'm not going to lose my son too. Either you get hold of Patrick or, or..."

Jean cries softly, "I will, I will. Please, I will, I promise."

Joan states, "I hope so, Jean, because I've tried and he gives me that 'you're-not-my-mother' stare."

Jean pleads, "Maybe Uncle John could get a little more involved."

"You know he's always said, 'Don't come crying to me if your kids break the law just cuz' I'm a cop.' I don't know how much he wants to get involved," Joan is quick to point out.

Karma

Jean says "I'll call him anyway, maybe he can come over before work tomorrow and have breakfast with us."

Joan replies, "Well, you can ask."

Next morning. Newspaper hits the front door. Joan opens door and retrieves it. Reads aloud, "Bank branch blown up. Police say they found a glove which belongs to a suspect." Patrick runs to his coat to check pockets for gloves. Finds only one.

There is loud knocking at the door. Joan opens it and is surprised by the police.

Police take Patrick out of the house in handcuffs. His Uncle John (brother to his mother and aunt) is hugging Patrick's mother who is hysterical.

Nick thinks back to the court drama. Judge brings down gavel and states, "Fifteen years." Nick is in the row behind Patrick. Patrick turns and they lock eyes.

Chapter Four Nick Reflects on an Old Confession

Nick remembers the old cathedral with large stained glass windows. One of many beautiful architectural achievements scattered throughout Chicago.

Nick slides into the confessional. "Father you have to help me. I blew up that bank with Patrick! My Uncle John, the cop, said he was a minor and considering the horrible situation with the recent death of his father and his mother getting evicted from her house with Patrick, the courts probably wouldn't throw the book at him. Maybe just a couple of years and probation. But they sentenced him to fifteen years, Father!"

(Nick now crying profusely)

Nick cries, "I have to turn myself in, Father!"

Priest trying to calm Nick, "Now calm down, Nick. Things aren't always black and white. A terrible thing has happened, and Patrick's mother's heart is broken. What good would it do to turn yourself in and break your parents' hearts? You are both very bright boys. You can do right by Patrick by being the best student and person you can be. You can go to college and make something of yourself. It doesn't benefit anyone for 2 young boys to be sitting in jail for fifteen years."

Nick still sobbing, "Father, what should I do?"

Priest replies, "My son, you both did a terrible thing. By God's grace no one was hurt. You can help Patrick out by helping both of your families now.

Nick sobs, "But I should be punished, Father."

The Priest says quietly, "You will be; you have to live with this for the rest of your life. I absolve you of your sin. For your penance, I want you to pray for Patrick every day until he gets out. A well-led life out of jail may give a sense of purpose to Patrick. "

Karma

Chapter Five Nick Back at Office

Rap on door brings Nick back to present.

Tess, his plump secretary, appears at the door. "Mail, Nick. Business and a bunch of charity organizations. Are you on everybody's chump list? Do you give money to all these people?" Tess has been his secretary for a number of years and is loyal to a fault. She is middle-aged and thinks of Nick as a son and is very protective of him. She know there is a sadness and guilt about him but does not know why.

Nick laughs.

Tess continues, "Look at this picture of this poor guy with no arms and they're teaching him to paint with his nose. You're nuts! They probably have that guy locked in a shed and take him out for a picture to send to suckers like you. Then they party in Tahiti with the suckers' money!"

Nick still laughing, "Tess, you are all heart baby, all heart."

Nick looks at time on computer, 11:45, and jumps up, puts on his coat, heads out of building to The Palm.

Karma

Chapter Six Lunch at The Palm

Very swanky sky scrapers. The restaurant is on the first floor. Big windows showcase bustling traffic and shoppers.

Waiters in coat and tails. Tables and booths in dark mahogany set with linen table cloths, china plates, crystal glasses, and silver silverware.

Joan walking past the restaurant carrying shopping bags and sees Uncle John through the window. They both wave, and Joan walks into the restaurant.

Joan walks up to Uncle John's table. "Fancy seeing you here. Did you win the lotto?"

Uncle John replies, "Actually, I'm meeting your son here for lunch, and he's paying."

Joan sits down. "Mind if I sit and wait till he comes?"

"No, no, have a seat, by all means," John returns.

Joan looks around as it to measure her words. "Will you be discussing Patrick?"

Uncle John, "I expect so. He's getting out tomorrow."

Joan sighs wearily, "Yes I know. I wish Jean were here to see it."

Uncle John, "We all wish that...She was all heart all her life and I think that's what killed her, you know? Just a broken heart."

Joan replies, "Yeah, sometimes I think she was my polar opposite, but we were twins. It was like she got all the goodness." She pauses and looks at John. Joan continues, "Well?"

Uncle John, "Well what?"

Joan attacks, "You agree with that?"

Uncle John defending himself, "Well, yeah. She was the good one and you were the bitch," he says jokingly. "Did you expect me to argue with that?"

Karma

Joan rolls her eyes. "You know, Nick's life has really been affected by this crap too. He walks around with some kind of complex, and he won't commit to a relationship. I mean I'd like some grandkids someday."

John comes back, "Is it always about you?"

Joan replies, "Oh and what do you think about all day, Retired Cop, Mr. Bachelor? Let's see...fishing trips, Kentucky Derby, Arlington Race Track all summer. *Pfff*. Anyway, it's not about me; it's about grandkids. There's nothing wrong with my wishing I could have some."

John more softly, "No, of course there isn't. I'm sorry, Joan. You comin' to the welcome home party at Glascott's?"

Joan sees Nick coming. Joan says quickly, "You know I wouldn't miss it." Joan slides over to get out then wages her finger at John. "Now don't you be stickin' my son with a big lunch bill, don't be gettin' the surf and turf!"

Not to be outdone, Uncle John retorts, "It's the drinks that kill you on the bill, Joan, and I plan on having several Tanqueray martinis."

Nick comes to the table, and Joan hugs him.

Joan accuses, "What have you been up to? You haven't answered my calls in three days!"

Nick defends, "Sorry, Ma. I've been real busy, but we'll catch up at Patrick's welcome home party."

Joan slyly asks, "Dating anyone nice?"

Nick answers, "No, I haven't met the love of my life since I last talked to you three days ago."

Joan replies, "Just asking. Okay you two, I'm off."

Nick and Uncle John together, "Bye."

Uncle John continues, "Boy, it'll be great to have Patrick back. You and he were always close when you were younger."

Nick answers, "We were quite the partners in crime. Most of the stuff we did, no one ever knew about."

Uncle John asks, "Like what?"

Nick says, "Well, I hate to incriminate myself, but I trust since all this is past the statute of limitations and you are a retired cop, there will be no backlash."

John laughing, "Well, aside from something like murder, I would agree."

Nick continues, "No nothing that exciting, just a couple of punks havin' fun, mostly on the weekends and summer vacations since this was all stuff done at night, and during the school year we always had our curfew with Dad."

John says, "Sure, your dad could be pretty strict."

Nick again, "Well, we started out small—throwing rocks at the lights in the Dominick's parking lot. We used to snap off the sprinkler heads at the different apartments and townhouses."

John asks, "Why do punks always have to be so destructive?"

Nick shrugs, "I don't know. I think it's just the age group; you don't really realize how much you're inconveniencing the older people. Next, we moved on to helping ourselves to anything inside cars that weren't locked. I always let Patrick take the risk with a couple of other friends that were as fearless as he was. I would be the lookout guy."

John interested asks, "Wow! Anything else?"

Nick continues, "Oh sure, then we started joyriding the cars. He had a friend whose grandfather was a mechanic and taught him quite a lot about cars. Dylan would hot wire the cars, Patrick would drive, and the rest of us would go along for the ride."

John states, "If your father knew half the crap you kids pulled, he would have kicked your ass into tomorrow."

Karma

Nick says, "That's an understatement. And then there was the time Patrick took a Volkswagen stick shift, which he had no idea how to drive, out on the highway and then bragged about stopping for gas with a cop right at the gas station. It was just Patrick and Dylan that time."

John asks, "Why do you think he always took such outrageous risks? That really sounds quite dangerous. He could have killed someone or himself."

Nick responds, "I don't know; we just thought it was funny. I think his brain was just different. Nowadays he probably would be medicated for ADHD or something like that. Now that I'm older, I'll always feel guilty for taking advantage of him like that and letting him take the risks."

John says, "Well, you never got caught, so nothing to feel guilty about."

Nick slips," What about the bank?" It was out before he realized it.

Uncle John looks sharply. "What about it? I thought you had nothing to do with that. I always suspected though."

Nick was flushed and started to look very uncomfortable. "Some things are just better left between you and your confessor."

John responds, "Okay, Nick, don't mean to pry. I know you really suffered after Patrick went away; you two were like brothers. Your mother told me you cried yourself to sleep for months after Patrick left."

Nick says quickly, "Well, that's all in the past. Now, it's time to celebrate, and I'm going to help Patrick out any way I can."

John shouts, "I'll drink to that!"

Chapter Seven Nick's Present-Day Confession

Nick is with the priest in confessional before he is going to pick up Patrick from prison.

Nick blesses himself, "Bless me Father, I never thought this day would come. I go to pick Patrick up from prison tomorrow."

Priest answering, "Why so low? This should be a great day!"

Nick starts to sob profusely. "Father, it's not fair. Patrick was in prison for the last fifteen years while I've had a successful career."

Priest answers again, "Now listen here, Nick, you've been in your own private prison for the last fifteen years. Time to forgive yourself; God has."

Nick sobs, "Okay, Father, you always know the right thing to say. I guess it comes from years of practice in the confessional."

Priest responds, "That and a little divine inspiration. Go in peace, Nick, and celebrate the reunion with your cousin."

Karma

Chapter Eight Picking up Patrick from Jail

The scenery shows monolithic concrete buildings surrounded by fences topped with barbed wire. Upon moving closer, over the fence, past the guard tower that is a pentagon shape, to the front door, and into the jail. The guard is behind the desk. Patrick is in front of the desk to receive his belongings from when he first went to jail.

The jailer quips, "Here's your stuff, Pat: pair of Keds, Members Only Jacket, two dollars and thirty-one cents, and a Ninja Turtle?"

Patrick replies, "He was my lucky totem."

Jailer comes back, "You ended up in here pal, so how lucky could he have been?"

Patrick says, "Yeah, that's true, but I'm still standin'."

Pat walks out of jail and sees Nick and Uncle John waiting in front of John's Hyundai. Hugs and teary eyes all around.

Patrick asks, "You still have that old car, John?"

John answers, "Four hundred thousand miles and still runs great. Why mess with success?"

Patrick says quickly, "Let's go. Faster I get away from here the better."

Nick, choking back tears, just nods.

John says, "I wish your mom was here to see this."

Patrick comes back, "She sees me all right, and I pray to her every night."

"Yeah, I'm sure she's up there looking out for you. There's a party at Glascott's and everyone from the old hood will be there," says John.

Karma

Chapter Nine Party at Glascott's

Crowded, noisy with laughter and cheers. Back slapping, congrats. Long oak bar—longest bar in Chicago—Irish music playing.

Nick comments, "At least they don't have the bagpipers."

Patrick chimes in, "I'm so happy I would even do a hornpipe."

Nick smiles, "Why were you practicing your Irish step-dancing skills in the joint? I bet the other prisoners enjoyed that."

Joan races up. "Hey guys, I got a joke. Now, it's pretty good, but it's kinda racy."

Patrick says, "Racy? There's a word I haven't heard in what, fifteen years."

Joan starts out her joke, "Okay, Okay, so there's a priest assigned to his first parish, and he's hearing confessions for the first time. Every other guy that comes in confesses to having unholy thoughts about Pussy Green. Then the next day during Sunday Mass, this buxom blonde makes her way up the center aisle, sits right in the first pew, and spreads her legs. The priest bends down to the altar boy and whispers, 'Is that Pussy Green?' The altar boy whispers back, 'No Father, I think that's just the reflection of the stained glass windows.'"

Loud laughter erupts after the joke.

Joan starts in again, "Got another one. Two Irish women, Molly and Sarah, are picking potatoes. Molly, holding two potatoes, all of a sudden starts to cry. Sarah says in an Irish brogue, 'Molly, why are ya cryin' now?' Molly replies, 'It's just that these potatoes remind me of my late husband's balls.' Sarah says, 'Oh! They were that big then?' Molly says, 'No, that dirty.'"

Laughter again after the joke.

Karma

Now Nick, getting a little under the weather, says to Pat, "I've never thanked you proper for takin' all the blame."

Patrick replies, "What would be the point of us both goin' away? Besides, it was me and my mom who got screwed over by the bank."

Nick argues, "But I was there too. I helped with everything. You couldn't have put together the explosives."

Patrick waving his hand to dismiss. "So, Nick, do you have a special someone in your life?"

Nick says, "No, just a hookup. She spends the night sometimes. She's married to her job."

Patrick says enthusiastically, "What about your job? You running the place? You always were the smart one."

Nick comes back, " No, but I have a job."

Patrick asks, "Hobbies? Passions?"

Nick says dryly, "I stay out of trouble and that's good enough for me."

Patrick shouts, "What's wrong with you? You act like you've been in prison for fifteen years—one you've made for yourself. I always imagined you having fun out here, and it made me feel good. Now I see you're just a downtrodden spirit of a man!"

Nick goes to restroom. He is washing his hands incessantly. Patrick comes in, observes Nick washing his hands, and comments, "You scrubbin' for surgery, Chief?" Patrick uses bathroom, rinses hands, and goes back out to the bar.

A couple of girls they hired for Pat's homecoming do a couple of Irish dances. After this, Pat has another dance with a beautiful girl. They dance to a modern-day song.

Girl dancer comments, "Where have you been, handsome?"

Patrick answers honestly, "I've been out of town."

Uncle John is seated at a table with Nick, and Patrick saunters over to join them.

Uncle John asks, "What's goin' on boys? You havin' fun? Pat, you're stayin' with me. I got the couch all set up for you, and we'll see your parole officer tomorrow. It's a buddy of mine."

Patrick says, looking dazed, "I look around at all these people and I don't know them; everybody looks so old. Do I look so old? Fifteen years, fifteen years."

John states, "The funny thing is, if you blew up a bank today, people would be lining up to pin a medal on you."

Patrick remarks, "So I hear, so I hear."

John continues, "Especially since they deregulated the banks. The bastards really went to town with the CMOs, CDOs and CLOs—Wall Street slicing and dicing loans and investments. They became so complex, no one could figure their worth. And the way they pay their guys—they get bonuses of millions if they can show on paper they made money but don't get punished if they lose. It's called lack of moral hazard. The guys working Wall Street stole like an employee of a place of business, just stealing the merchandise."

Pat and Nick looking with mouths agape.

Patrick asks, "CMO what?"

Karma

John answers, "Collateralized mortgage obligations, collateralized debt obligations, and collateralized loan obligations."

Pat and Nick look at each other and back at John with confused looks.

John says, "What? I'm retired and got time to read. I even have a library card."

Nick asks, "But do you understand?"

John answers, "Takes a lot of thinkin', but that's the point. Those Wall Street guys want us all to say, 'We don't get it,' then they steal like crazy. I'm an ex-cop - I understand robbin' and stealin'. Every pension fund in the country—teachers, firemen, police, etc.—got sent down to Wall Street to get invested. These jerks lost the money while paying themselves millions, and now they are saying people were promised too much from their pensions."

Patrick asks, "Do you get that, Nick?"

Nick says, "Yes, as a matter of fact I do. I'm just amazed Uncle John, who likes to watch fishing shows and wrestling on T.V., gets it."

John charges, "What? That's the only thing on T.V. worth watching and besides, Nick, where do you think you got your brains?"

Patrick asks, "Yeah, Nick, you got brains, and it would be great if we could steal some of this money back. They probably have a lot of it hidden in secret bank accounts so nobody can get at it. I bet those banks got all kinds of ways to hide stolen money."

Joan walking by, overhears. Joan yells out, "Patrick, you just got out and you're gonna get MY son in trouble?" She stomps audibly off.

John asks, "What about that Patriot Act that they passed? Doesn't it let the USA look at every secret account, on account of the terrorists, to see who's been funding them?"

Patrick is incredulous. "The banks just handed this secret info to the U.S.?"

Nick explains, "Well, we threatened them a little, so they say. So they say to Switzerland, 'You better release your account info so we can see who's funding terrorists, or you better check your army.'"

Patrick says, "Ya, they better have something better than that Swiss Army knife. Like that's scary." He continues in a Swiss accent, "Watch out or I'll open your beer can and file your nails!"

Nick continues, "Yeah that's right, but we promised we'd only act against the bank and seize assets when it was terrorism; otherwise, we're supposed to look the other way."

Patrick says sarcastically, "Supposed to huh? And you always do what you're supposed to do? Don't you work for the good old USA? Can't you get in there and see?"

Nick scoffs, "They'd be on me like a stink on shit. They would know who was looking, and I'd be in cuffs in two hours after getting in."

Patrick pushes, "Sleep on it, cousin, and sleep is what I want now too. I'm not used to all this Jameson. You didn't liquor me up just to take advantage of me, Uncle John, did you?"

Karma

Chapter Ten Wrigley Field Six Months Later

Two guys are in the bleachers in front of Nick and Pat.

First guy comments, "I bet he spits to the left."

Second guy answers, "You're on."

Pitchers spits to the left before winding up.

First guy says excitedly, "That's a beer you owe me."

Patrick comments, "There's nothing like a hot dog and a cold one at the game! I remember when these bleacher seats were a dollar."

"You HAVE been away a long time! Yeah, the little guy can't afford to bring his kid to a game anymore," answers Nick.

Short silence.

Patrick starts slowly," You think about that thing we talked about? I can't get a job and I looked and looked and you owe me. Guys with college degrees and halos on their heads can't find work. I hear they bailed the bank bastards out with seven hundred fifty billion dollars. Allan Brownstreak, Harry Paulsin, Dick Folded, Jake Demon, Harry Patel, Robbie Rube, Aaron Holdit, to name a few, and what was that company's name that insured them all, A something...AIG?"

Girls in back of Pat and Nick as organist plays a tone.

First girl, "Mr. Sandman."

Second girl, "You always win at name that tune!"

First girl, "That's a bag of peanuts you owe me."

Pat laughs at the two girls behind them, then lowers his voice and says to Nick, "That Allan Brownstreak changed the rules so that the Harry

Karma

Paulsins and the Jake Demons of the world could rob us blind. How come they get away with it, and a poor guy like Edmond Snowday has to hide in Russia for exposing some truths about Big Brother watching?"

Nick comments, "You've been talking to Uncle John?"

Patrick continues, "Not just him, I've read some Nouriel Roubini too. These guys are just looters. They changed the rules so they could plunder money they were given to invest—pension funds too! You're supposed to get a pension, aren't ya? That was your money too, and nobody's doin' nothin'." Silence. "Can't you just hack in and steal a few million?"

Nick dryly, "Yeah, there's no way."

Patrick presses on, "You don't know anybody that could do it?"

Nick thinks on it. "I think I do, but the person isn't allowed near a computer; the government watches the ones who can bring it down."

Patrick continues, "There's gotta be a way. What's the name?"

Nick replies, "Toni. Toni can get around almost anything, incredible skill. Toni can hack into anything."

Patrick is getting excited. "Can you get in touch with him?"

Nick states, "Her. It's Antionette."

Patrick asks, "Really? What, she's so ugly she sits alone with her computer?"

Nick smiles and shakes his head. "No, she's pissed. Her mother was deported for driving without having a license when Toni 14, just before her Quinceañera. And her ma died in Mexico. I don't know where she is."

Patrick asks, "How do you know her?"

Nick brags, "I'm the one who found her. Fucked up the immigration computer pretty good. Hell of a hacker." Nick has a wistful look on his face.

Nick has a flashback of the scene where Toni was being questioned—only 15 and very pretty. He was always attracted to her.

Patrick keeps pressing, "Hell of a hacker and what else?"

Nick comes back from the flashback, "Nothin'. She was 15 and a criminal."

Patrick asks, "How long ago was that?"

Nick answers, "Six or seven years ago."

A home run ball from the opposing team is caught by Pat. Crowd is jeering at him to throw back the ball, and he does.

Karma

Chapter Eleven Toni's Apartment

A second story apartment building, bay windows in front with heavy yellow drapes, big stuffed couch and chair in shades of orange, old shag carpet. A Spanish tune is playing by Vicki Carr, "Coocorocoocoo, Paloma." In the background is a shrine for the Lady of Guadalupe. A beautiful young woman with straight black hair peeks out of window and sees a man. Squinting, she looks again. Then with a look of surprise, grabs her coat and goes outside.

Outside an old apartment building in the back of the yards. Nick across the street looking at the building. Beautiful twenty-something woman walks out, sees him, and walks over.

Toni says surprised, "Well, well, if it isn't ' Mr. Straight as an Arrow.' Thought you'd never come around here. Are you looking for me or just here to appreciate the back-of-the-yard ambiance?"

Nick stammers, "Well er, yes, er no. I, I'm, it's been a while since I last saw you. Seven years. I never guessed you'd be in the same place living with your grandmother."

Toni replies, "They'd find me wherever, so why not just stay with mi abuela? Still can't work with computers, can't get a job besides flippin' tortillas, and my parole officer still checks on my every now and then."

Nick asks, "So you're stayin' out of trouble?"

Toni charges, "Pretty hard to get in trouble these days. Can't talk to any of my old computer buddies, and to tell the truth, I don't care to. " Walking some more. "If it wasn't for mi abuela, I'd be in a crack house just lookin' for some happiness. I think I got me a case of that social anomie."

Nick asks, "You been reading some psychology?"

"No, just watchin' *'The Mob Wives'*," explains Toni.

Karma

Nick chuckling, "Well, you're a perfect candidate—super smart, feel the world is being so unfair. Lots of smart people just check out—drink, do drugs, whatever."

Toni states, "Yeah, those mob wives know life's unfair, but they somehow keep fightin'. I'm tired of it all too, but I've been prayin' a lot to La Señora de Guadalupe."

"Getting any answers?" Nick inquires.

Toni replies, "Maybe. You're here." Silence. "One thing I never figured out, Nick."

Nick says, "What's that?"

Toni charges, "Why'd you let your boss, that stupid ass with bad breath, take all the credit for tracking me down when I hacked into the Government Immigration Computer?"

Nick looks surprised. "How do you know he didn't?"

Toni simply states, "Because after two minutes I could tell his I.Q. was two points below snail shit, yet you acquiesce to him. You're a real case. What's the deal? Father beat you? Mother shame you? Something eating you?"

They continue to walk in silence. Nick growing uncomfortable.

Nick says, "Did I ever tell you about my cousin Pat? Well long story short, he and his mother had their house foreclosed on after Pat's father died. A very upset Pat blew up the bank and went away for fifteen years because of the deed."

Toni says surprised, "Blew up a bank, huh?"

Nick explains, "Well, just a bank branch actually."

Toni exclaims, "Boy, they'd give him a medal today!"

"Yeah, that seems to be the consensus," Nick agrees.

Toni starts thinking and realization dawns on her face. "What are we going to be up to, Nick?" Toni claps her hands with excitement.

Nick lowers his voice, "How closely are they watching you?"

Toni says dryly, "They've got bigger fish to fry. I just can't get a regular job with computers."

So Nick asks, "So what would you need to hack into the banks?"

Toni bites her lower lip thinking. "Well, they're all separate; you'd have to do it one at a time."

"Not necessarily. Ever hear of the Patriot Act?" Nick responds.

Toni, her mouth agape, "I never put that together. Do you mean all the banks are in one USA computer?"

Nick states, "That's what I'm saying. I could get in with my password but then they'd know it was me, and the cyber anti privacy is so good, you'd need a super computer to hack it without being detected."

Toni asks, "How about your boss' password?"

Nick smiles, "Yeah, you're not going to believe it, but he keeps it in his top drawer; the cleaning people could've gotten it by now. Just like in the movie *'Marnie'*."

Toni makes a face. "What a jerk, but good for us. If we get in the computer that has the secret bank accounts with his password, how soon would it be detected?"

"Just a day or two and then it would get fixed, and fatso would be arrested, but we wouldn't be able to keep the money, and they'd probably get us too," Nick explains.

Karma

Toni says, "It might be worth it just to see him in cuffs."

Nick scoffs, "No, it wouldn't, but you got any ideas? All I want to do is steal a million or so and not get caught. Give it to Pat and we'll be square."

"Just Pat?" asks Toni.

Nick replies sheepishly, "Well, some for you too. I figure these jerks broke the banks, brought down the world's economy, and they just got away with it. Nobody took *their* money back, no jail time, nothing!"

Toni looks surprised. "Yeah, why is that?"

Nick says, "Don't know. Not even a real investigation into it all. Maybe that's the point. If they did a real investigation, they might find the culprits."

Toni says seriously, "Well, I found out at a young age this world is an unfair place. The poor always pay the price. I would just like to turn the tables just once."

Nick says intently, "We're not gonna do all that. We're just going to steal a few million, just to make it fair for Pat...and you of course. The thing is, if it looks like the US computer that looks for terrorist money is the one removing a few million from an account, the bank won't bat an eye, and of course the US doesn't share any info they have on terrorism with the bank, so they won't care. We just have to keep the guys who watch the federal info computer from noticing that this is happening."

Toni says excitedly, "That's where I come in!"

Nick says, "Yeah, that's where I could use your help."

Toni demands, "Why don't you get your fat boss' password and just do it in the office?"

Nick explains, "It's too risky. I won't have the time to look at everything I want to."

"Why don't you get a new laptop, use it once to break in and then throw it away, the way the crooks do with throw away cell phone?" asks Toni.

Nick thinks, "That might work, we just need a location that has WiFi and no cameras. I know the perfect out-of-the-way coffee house. We'll have to use disguises though because of the cameras on the street."

Toni exclaims, "Hey, this is more fun than Halloween!"

Karma

Chapter Twelve The Coffeehouse

Nick and Toni are dressed up as an older couple, thinking this will be an unnoticeable disguise. Now driving, Nick parks on a side street a couple of blocks away.

Toni asks, "Why are we parking so far away?"

Nick answers, "We don't want any cameras on the main street getting my license plate."

They exit the car and start walking down the street toward the cafe.

Toni asks slowly, "So...how come you never got married?"

Nick throws the ball back, "I guess I could ask you the same thing."

"So dodging the question with another question?" asks Toni.

Nick confesses, "Well, I guess this whole business with Pat going to jail and living with the guilt has left me pretty emotionally unavailable."

Toni says softly, "Haven't you been a little hard on yourself?"

Nick replies, "I guess, but I really felt bad. So how about you, still searching for that perfect man?"

"I guess I've been looking for my soul mate, just like every other poor girl. I might have met him though," answers Toni.

Nick asks surprised, "Oh really, who is the lucky guy?"

Toni looks exasperated "Come on, Nick, you can't be that thick?"

Nick embarrassed says nothing. They finish walking in silence. Now in the cafe.

Karma

Nick says, "Two lattes please." He is careful not to make eye contact. Nick is now getting into the computer. "Okay, let's see what those boys were up to. Keying in Alan Brownstreak one hundred forty million in the Caymans. "

Toni asks, "Harry Paulson, is it with an *e* or an *o*?"

Nick responds sarcastically, "It's Paulsin with an *i* as in SIN."

Toni states, "Oh, there's our guy—one hundred million in the Caymans, Dick Folded, Jake Demon...looks like there's some big CEO names from European banks too."

Nick says, "None of our guys are in Switzerland or Israel or Germany or England, all in the Caymans. Holy shit! Not sure if you knew this or not, Toni, didn't see it on any news channels only on the Internet, and since you don't use computers anymore—"

Toni, running out of patience. "What are you talking about?"

Nick says evenly, "We not only bailed out the financial institutions for seven hundred fifty billion dollars, but since Congress passed a law allowing the Fed to be audited, it was discovered that sixteen trillion was taken and distributed to Wall Street and several banks in Europe. Why we had to bail out the banks in Europe with American hard-earned money is beyond me."

Toni says incredulously, "Why aren't the people rioting?"

Nick answers, "Since it wasn't on the regular news, I don't think a lot of people know. I think it's pretty shocking that they would take all our money and do this."

Toni demands, "Who let them do this?"

Nick explains, "The Fed is not regulated by our government, they have their own board and pretty much do as they like. That's the way they set it up back in 1913. Okay, the Fed does reflect that sixteen trillion was given to these various institutions. But I guess the CEOs skimmed six trillion right off the top. That's roughly the same amount that made its way into the Caymans in the same timeframe."

Toni exclaims, "My God, those greedy bastards!"

"There really shouldn't be all this money tied up," says Nick.

"What's it mean?" asks Toni.

Nick replies, "I don't recognize any of the other account holders and actually, I figured the guys we know would have one hundred million or so in these accounts, but this adds up to trillions!"

Toni cries, "Greed, greed, and more greed! You'd think these guys would be afraid that one day they'll meet their maker!"

Nick says dryly," Maybe they're gonna be freeze-dried and brought back to life or some such crap."

"Okay, let's get out of here. I'm starting to feel sick!" exclaims Toni.

Walking back to the car with heads down.

Toni offers, "I'll keep the laptop at my place if you want."

Nick says a little too loudly," No! I don't want you to get in any trouble. I'll dispose of it myself."

Toni says, "Okay, okay."

Karma

Chapter Thirteen Uncle John's House

Uncle John's house is in St. Charles, a suburb of Chicago. Small Cape Cod style brick with an unfinished basement. The house is fairly messy but clean. Blinds, but not curtains. One wall hanging in the front room of mounted fish. Uncle John is not home.

Nick says to Pat, "You won't believe it, there's trillions in those secret accounts in the Caymans. The bailout for the banks was supposed to be seven hundred billion, but an additional sixteen trillion was used to bail out the same institutions with some European banks added in, and six trillion was used to set up a bunch of accounts in the Caymans. There's no way to hack in. The walls are really sealed."

Patrick asks surprised, "You mean it was in 'Inside Job'?"

Toni says ironically, "Really, corruption?"

Nick answers, "Not the regular guys who get elected, but there's so much secrecy with the Fed and now that it's been audited, the cat's out of the bag. But this money stuff is breaking the world's economy."

Pat exclaims, "Well, let's steal it back!"

Silence.

Pat comes back, "Well, why not?"

Nick asks, "And what would we do with it, the trillions?"

Pat explains, "Redistribute it, back to the bank accounts!"

Nick says, "I don't know, we'll have to think about that. Not sure if that could be done."

Toni thinking, "I guess I could come up with an algorithm with every bank account, say under fifty thousand, and divide it up that way."

Karma

Nick thinking, "I don't know. How would we notify the people?"

Toni says, "We can figure the logistics later. Maybe send the account holders a message signed 'Robin Hood'?"

Pat cried, "That would be so cool and really the fair thing to do!"

Nick says, "All right, we'll figure the logistics later, but seems like a pipedream because I'm not sure how we could break in."

Toni exclaims, "We'll just have to build our own supercomputer!"

Nick scoffs, "That would do it. Sure, we'll just build a super computer and solve the world's problems."

Toni ignores him, "I was playing with my cousin's PlaysStation 3 and it's a kickass computer.

Nick thinking, "We could string a bunch of them together like two hundred or so..."

Toni remarks, "Yeah, kind of like many hands make light work. My mother used to say that; it's a Mexican saying."

Patrick chimes in, "My mother used to say that too."

Toni adds, "See how much we Mexicans have influenced your American culture?"

"You're nuts!" Pat exclaims.

Nick steps in, "Okay you two, knock it off. Remember we're supposed to stick together if we are gonna pull anything off."

Pat thinking, "So, two hundred PlayStations. Where you gonna get so many PlayStation 3s? I think you might need some criminals." Looking pleased with himself.

Nick stares. "Don't do anything yet, Pat, we don't know what or if or when we're gonna do this."

"Okay," Pat agrees.

Karma

Chapter Fourteen Back at the Coffee Shop

Two FBI agents are in the coffee shop questioning the owner. It's a small but quaint little coffee shop with a lot of ambience. A lot of regulars from the neighborhood frequent the shop.

Agent One asks, "Do you remember who was in here last night using a laptop?"

Owner of coffee shop replies, "Just an elderly couple. Didn't notice the woman, she was sitting over there. The gentleman had very nice manners though, about medium height and build. I think he had glasses too. His voice sounded familiar though."

Both FBI agents look at each other and say at the same time, "They used a disguise."

Agent Two hands his card to the owner and says, "If you think of anything else or see them again, please call me."

Owner says, "Will do."

They hurry out of the shop looking grim and very businesslike.

Karma

Chapter Fifteen Back at Nick's Office

Back at the office, Nick notices several 'FBI looking men' ushering Alan, Nick's boss, to a separate office and start questioning him.

Alan, perspiring and nervous asks, "What's this? Wwwwhat are you doing?" Stuttering all over the place.

FBI Agent One, "Oh, I think you know."

Still stammering Alan says, "Nnno, I don't know, what is ggoing on?"

FBI Agent Two, "Why were you checking the Patriot Act Computer?"

Alan looks shocked. "I nnever look at that unless I have a direct order."

FBI Agent One, "We have you logged in yesterday."

Alan feverishly denies, "I ddidn't!"

FBI Agent Two, "Who would know your password? Opening his drawer. What's this Alan? You careless lazy mother fucker! Nobody's that dumb! What an act Alan! Left it right in the open, so even the janitor could break in! What a huge security breach!"

FBI Agent One, "Nobody is that stupid. The big guy is gonna love this! What an idiot!"

Alan is speechless.

Tess comes over to Nick, who is pretending not to notice.

Tess asks, "What's going on with Alan? I heard some of those guys screaming at Alan, something about keeping his password in his top drawer and what an idiot he is."

Nick looks surprised, "He really does that? He IS an idiot."

Karma

Tess exclaims, "Looks like they're ushering him out of the building. Boy is Alan's face red! "

Men all walk past Nick and Tess with Alan looking like he lost his last friend.

Tess continues, "If he goes I guess you'll take over for Alan, right? You always did all the work, Nick. You deserve it!"

Nick tries to be uninterested, "Well, let's not jump the gun. I guess we'll just have to wait and see what's going on."

Nick tries to look naive and innocent but is perspiring. The whole office is abuzz. Nick calls Patrick.

Nick speaks softly into the phone, "We need to meet. The heat is on already. We can't meet at my place and of course not at Toni's. They may be watching me now."

Patrick says quickly, "Come to Uncle John's, they know you usually go there, and he's off on a fishing trip."

"That might be good," says Nick. Nick, using a payphone, calls Toni and tells her to go to Uncle John's and lay low.

Chapter Sixteen Uncle John's Basement

It's late afternoon, and they all meet at Uncle John's while he's out of town. Patrick is whooping and hollering.

"Yeah, I know some great thieves. My best friends as a matter of fact," explains Patrick.

Nick asks, "You met them in the joint? That doesn't speak highly of their skills if they got caught."

Patrick explains, "It's booze or drugs that caused them to be reckless and get punished."

"How could we rely on them then," Nick presses him.

Patrick replies, "They're not stupid; they'll be cool when they have a job to do. It's just when they don't, they get into trouble. They're the kind of guys who need, I don't know. I just know how to handle 'em. But how much money are we gonna steal?"

Nick states, "Actually, Pat, we're not gonna steal it, okay. We'll steal plenty, but what we're gonna do is redistribute the wealth. Take it from the personal accounts of the jagoffs that did this, you know. The Alan Brownstreaks and Dick Folds and the Paulsins of the world. Just redistribute it. It's not that I'm a socialist. I just think capitalism is supposed to be more fair, and it's just these kinds of thieves that will lead the world to communism. I think these guys started out to be good guys, and I'm sure they thought they were good men. How they ended up where they did is beyond me."

"Well, I've hung out with some bad guys for fifteen years. Most of 'em had lousy breaks all their lives, but these jerks had everything," observes Pat.

Nick replies, "Obviously they didn't think so. I think it starts with one tiny lie and over time builds and builds till you don't know the truth anymore or just don't care."

Karma

Toni walks in with donuts and has heard.

She remarks, "Remember cancer starts with just one cell."

Nick comments, "Yeah that's just what this is, and we're gonna administer the chemotherapy. Now tell me about your guys from the inside. "

Pat starts to explain, "There's George, an accountant jailed for fraud. I guess he's got a Swiss bank account or something that they never found. " Shows picture of him cuffed at his desk. "He was my first friend inside. Then there is Jeff, expert thief. He can dismantle any alarm. Steals jewels mostly. Got pinched when a jilted girlfriend turned him in." Shows Jeff crawling out of the jewelry store back window and cops standing there waiting for him. "And then there's good old Whitey, not brilliant but loyal to the core. He'll do whatever I tell him."

Nick asks, "Can you get these guys? They all out now?"

Pat brags, "I got 'em."

Nick surprised, "You what?"

Pat continues, "I got 'em; they're on the way over here. I can read your mind, man."

Shave-and-a-haircut-two-bits-knock on the door.

Nick looks, "What, a secret knock?" he ironically asks.

Pat opens the door and in steps George, hugs and introductions.

George smiles and eyes Toni. "Well hello, honey. So what's this all about? This your cousin Nick you told me about?"

Pat answers, "Yeah it is."

George goes on, "You know the story of Pat's first week in prison? Let me tell you. He comes in little blue-eyed blonde. Fifteen years old with 'bitch' written on his back, you know? Next morning at breakfast, throws his tray at the baddest mother f'er and then takes his cock-eyed boxer stance. He creamed this guy who outweighed him by at least seventy pounds. "

Pat laughs, "Yeah those boxing lessons with my dad paid off."

Nick comments, "I guess it helped that your dad was a Golden Gloves winner plus the fact that you never, never quit, always keep comin' and comin'."

George says, "Yeah he never backs down almost to a fault. But anyways, back then I had a habit that I picked up in prison. Pat helped me put it down. I'd get paroled then somewhere down the line I'd get fouled up and get pinched for something stupid."

Nick asks, "You clean now? I mean, can you stay clean?"

George raises his brows, "I'm working with you? No problem, no problem."

Another knock at the door. A man with white-blonde hair walks in with large buttocks from working out.

George yells out, "Whitey, my man. You need to lay off the squats, man!"

Pat laughing, "Yeah, we heard your butt cheeks smackin' together before we saw you."

Whitey explains, "I'm keepin' myself busy okay? I gotta keep busy! So good to see you guys again. What's it been, three months since I got out? Haven't seen Georgie in about a year. How you doin', man?" Shakes George's hand. Seeing Toni, "Who's this? What a looker!"

Toni snaps, "I'm the brains here so don't be getting any ideas!"

Nick says, "I'm Nick, Pat's cousin." He reaches out to shake his hand.

Another knock, door opens.

Karma

Patrick excitedly says, "Get in here. This is my man Jeff who can get whatever you need wherever it is."

Jeff says, "You hopin' that, anyway."

They all settle in. There's the sound of door opening upstairs and slamming. Everyone in the basement freezes and questioning eyes all dart at Nick.

Nick whispers, "Shh, I'll go see."

Toni softly, "Me too."

Nick argues, "No, stay here. I'll go alone."

Nick goes upstairs. Joan hears a noise and screams loud and long. She sees that it is Nick.

Joan demanding, "What are you doing here? You scared me to death!"

Nick also demanding, "What are you doing here? You scared me!"

Joan explains, "I'm here to water the plants while your uncle is away."

Nick asks, "Since when does Uncle John have plants?"

"Since I gave him some. They give off oxygen, and they brighten the place up," Joan explains.

Nick asks again, "And he gave you a key to the place?"

Joan answers, "Of course, it's not like I'm going to have a wild party here!"

Nick responds, "Oh I don't know, those jokes you told at the party were pretty 'racy'." Nick uses air quotes when he says racy.

Joan asks again, "Now, what are you doing here?"

Just then Toni comes upstairs, Joan sees her and eyes her up and down clearly noticing how beautiful Toni is.

Joan is stunned, "Who is this?"

Nick answers, "This is Toni, Mother. Toni, this is my mother."

Toni says, "Pleased to meet you, Mrs. Cusack."

Joan replies, "Likewise. Have you two known each other for a while?"

Nick and Toni answer at the same time.

Nick says, "No, we just met."

Toni says, "Oh yes, a long time."

Joan raises her eyebrows.

Joan demands, "Well, which is it?"

Nick says first, "Well, I've known her for a long time."

Toni adds, "I guess I've known who he was."

Joan looks confused, "Who he was?"

Toni says quickly, "You know, where he worked."

Nick cuts in, "But we just started seeing each other."

Joan's attitude changes a little and with a big smile says, "Seeing each other! You're such a pretty thing too!"

Toni blushes, "Thank you, you look great yourself, in fact, I would have taken you to be Nick's sister and not his mother."

Nick flashes Toni a look.

Karma

Joan responds, "Oh thank you, thank you. You wouldn't believe it but I hear that all the time. I want to invite you to dinner sometime, Toni. Would that be all right?"

Toni says, "That would be lovely. Yes, I'd love to come."

Nick cuts in, "All right, that's settled. Actually what we were doing here is—"

Toni quickly, "Hanging out. I live with my grandmother and…"

Joan says, "Well, I'll just be a minute here."

Toni says quickly, "Oh, we can water that plants."

Nick chimes in, "Yes, Mom, we can water the plants."

Joan replies, "Okay, Okay, you two just hang out. And how about dinner next Sunday?"

Nick, "Sounds good."

Toni, "Yes, I would love it."

Joan leaves with a big smile on her face. "Okay then." Once outside she says to herself, "Hanging out in the basement? The basement isn't finished." She shakes her head.

Back in the basement.

George inquires, "So, Nick, you say there's six trillion in hidden accounts? How could that be?"

Nick explains, "They took sixteen trillion out of the Federal Reserve, not just seven hundred billion from the Treasury. And six trillion is sitting in private accounts in the Caymans."

Pat scrunches up his face, "How much is that?"

Toni remarks, "A billions seconds is thirty years, so ya figure."

George observes, "I guess these jerks weren't gonna get caught with their pants down again. When the Great Depression hit, the big boys lost their money too. I guess this time they wised up and hid their stash."

Nick comments, "THEIR stash? Yeah, they hid it real good."

Toni starts to talk excitedly, "Well, what I need is some components to build a super computer. We'll hack in everywhere we want without a trace, theoretically at least. Maybe even a quantum physics computer, still thinking of that. You know, regular computers operate on binary code—zeroes and ones. If you split a like property, like a beam of light per quantum physics theory, the particles are now opposite. What if you could have a zero and one at the same time, processing data simultaneously, could speed up that processing time exponentially, no? We'd have to have fiber-optic processors though to split the beam of light . Anyways just a thought. Might be fun to try it out."

Nick looks surprised. "I thought you couldn't work with computers anymore."

Toni looks smug. "Yeah, but I can still watch Public Broadcasting T.V. Ever hear of it?"

Nick replies, "They don't teach this stuff on Public Broadcasting T.V."

Toni waves her hand dismissively. "They do if you pay attention— quantum physics week. I guess you missed it. Okay, so this is what we need, first about two hundred PlayStations, then need to convert the processors to fiber optic if it's going to be a quantum physics computer, so we can split the beam of light. This will mimic the zeroes and ones, the binary code that a computer works off of. Nick and I are going to work on that. Then just split the beam of light and presto, 'Super Computer'!"

Nick scratches his head. "Well, we hope it will be that easy."

Karma

Pat pipes up, "Okay, Jeff and Whitey, you guys are gonna steal the PlayStations. You can handle that right?"

Jeff answers, "Me? You know I can."

Toni quips, "Okay you guys, just don't get Ned Stark'd."

Pat asks, "Ned what?"

Toni explains, "*Game of Thrones*, HBO, end of season one. The only honest guy gets his head chopped, poor naive soul!"

Chapter Seventeen Stealing the PlayStations

Whitey and Jeff are driving a big blue van traveling down the highway. They are on their way to a warehouse to steal the two hundred PlayStations.

Whitey asks, "So you cased the place where we're gonna steal the Play Stations and can jam the alarms?"

Jeff says dryly, "Yeah, they're mickey mouse, no problem. We'll just pull into the loading dock, get in there, and load 'em up. Turn right here, I want to make a stop."

Whitey looks, questioning, "Into the 7-Eleven?"

Jeff says shortly, "Yeah, I need something."

Whitey presses him, "What?"

"Just pull in," Jeff insists.

Jeff goes into the 7-Eleven. Beautiful black girl with Muslim scarf at the counter. Name tag says "Miriam". Jeff who is obviously attracted to her says, "How you doin' tonight?"

Miriam replies, "Just fine." She looks at him and goes right back to cleaning the counter. Jeff gets bottle of pop and brings it to the counter.

Miriam asks, "That's it?" Very businesslike. "Same as this morning."

Jeff says, "Yeah, that's it. I like this Cherry Coke." Takes his time with his change, looks like he'd like to ask her out, but doesn't.

Miriam suggests, "Maybe you should buy a six-pack instead of coming in a few times a day to buy just one. And it's cheaper that way."

Jeff says sheepishly, "I guess it would be." Looking embarrassed, he leaves.

Karma

Out in the car, Whitey is waiting. Jeff gets in, and Whitey asks, "You get me one?"

Jeff says, "No man, sorry."

Whitey suggests, "Well now that we're here, I'm hungry. I'm getting me a hot dog." He goes into the 7-Eleven and returns with three hot dogs.

Jeff looks surprised. "Wow! I guess you were hungry."

They start to drive. Whitey wolfs down two hot dogs and lets out a loud burp. "I hate people who go fifty-five in the left lane—that passive-aggressive bullshit." Whitey looking very aggravated.

Jeff says sarcastically, "Yeah where's the highway sniper when you need him?"

Whitey, "Right?"

They exit back into loading dock of a warehouse. Jeff jumps out, disables the alarm, and opens the door. Holding door, Jeff says, "After you." Jeff yells, "Oh shit, it's a dog. Come on, Whitey!" Running out.

Inside Whitey doesn't move, and dog rushes past him to go out the door to get to Jeff. Jeff slams the door. Inside warehouse, Whitey is with the dog. Whitey sees the chain where the dog was. Whitey takes a relaxed stance. Whitey says softly, "Okay there boy, no one's gonna hurt you." Whitey calms down dog and yells to Jeff, "Go and get that last hot dog!" Jeff returns with it, Whitey gives it to the dog and chains him back up. They unload two hundred PlayStations and take off.

Chapter Eighteen Back in Uncle John's Basement

Back in Uncle John's basement, finds Toni and Nick building the super computer. They trip over each other trying to get to the computer.

George muses, "You can't have a secret bank account anymore if you're American. Some of the banks from foreign countries are afraid of the US. Anyone with US citizenship and with foreign bank accounts are being told they will let the US know of the accounts, so they can be taxed. So these guys are not US citizens."

He continues, "They're not US citizens if they want to hide in Switzerland, Israel, or anywhere almost. The US is telling these banks that they won't be allowed to invest in our stock market or commodities markets if they have US investors who are not paying taxes."

Patrick states, "So, who cares? The stock markets are down anyway."

George insists, "They care very much. They want to buy our bonds when everything else looks bad. I know Israel is telling all their American depositors to withdraw their funds, and Switzerland just gave the US six hundred eighty million dollars just to go away, and they're telling their American depositors to get out." Brief silence. "But! The Caymans doesn't care 'cuz they don't invest in our market anyway. The real thieves have their money in the Caymans!"

Nick asks, "So you think they are false identities?"

George thinks, "Could be anything, but if they are fake, it will be even easier to steal it. Who are they going to complain to?"

"All the more reason to use a super computer so it can't be traced. These guys wouldn't go to the law," Nick comments.

Pat interjects, "If these guys are outlaws at this level, they would never go to the law. They'd have their own hired army of guys to inflict hurt."

Karma

Toni, looking a little scared but trying to be brave says, "Well they can't trace a super computer. They just can't, right?" Looking at Nick.

Nick states emphatically, "Of course they can't. We just gotta build it."

Pat asks, "All we can do is get you the stuff you need. Can't help with the building of it. How's it gonna work again?"

Toni explains again, "First, Nick and I need to replace these processors with fiber-optic processors. Then for the quantum physics part, the light beam or photon will be split. When it splits, its properties will then be opposite. Computers talk computer language, binary code, zeroes, and ones. If the code, light beam is split, it can now be a zero and a one. This speeds up the processing power exponentially. It will be SUPER fast!"

Pat looks confused, "Does anybody really understand this?"

Toni answers, "Supposedly no, not even Einstein. He said it was spooky. No one knows why like properties after they are split apart, act differently. You know repressed, stifled," leans over to Nick, "hollow?"

Everyone in the room, eyes glued to Toni, waiting for the explanation.

Pat says smiling, "Are we still talking about quantum physics?"

Toni continues, "It's simple really. Quantum physics is about everything. If you separate something closely entangled that works together in nature and wasn't really supposed to be separate, then it goes against the laws of nature and it makes sense that they don't work without each other. It's like soul mates. When they're split apart, they just don't do very well without each other, no matter how far apart they are. "

George getting impatient, "Okay before we go off on a tangent, let's get this thing built."

Toni says, "It'll take Nick and I awhile. Let's meet here again in about a month. We'll let you know."

Before they get to work, Toni says, "That Occupy Wall Street, they have the right idea. Wall Street is the culprit, but they are going about it all wrong."

Nick looks puzzled. "Well, what would be right?"

Toni continues, "When the Twin Towers were hit, that was a blow against capitalism and free trade, but the people who benefitting the most from this, the one percent, were not asked to go and defend capitalism. Their spoiled sons were not asked to go and fight. The people who went to war were the people who signed up for the military to secure college funds. That's who defended capitalism. Anyone who lost a child, spouse, and parent in this war, should march on Wall Street and say, 'We made the ultimate sacrifice. What are you thieving pukes going to do? Our country is in financial trouble. Pay your fair share of taxes or haul your ass out of America. We won't defend your thieving anymore!'"

Nick suggests, "I thought you were mad at America."

Toni cries, "I am! They deport the wrong people. Kick out the Wall Street scum."

Nick says sullenly, "I'm afraid they are probably homegrown scum. We're stuck with them."

Toni says excitedly, "Then put them in prison! The people in Iceland took to the streets and protested and had the bankers thrown in jail. They also put the scoundrels in jail in Ireland. What are the people doing here? Everyone has their head in the sand, either that or they're watching *American Idol* or *America's Got Talent*. The people here haven't got a clue! And now they're talking about deregulating the banks again! Wake up, America!"

Nick says slyly, "Or just steal their money, the only thing they understand. I'm feeling better and better about what we're doing."

They get to work. Later, place is a mess.

Karma

Chapter Nineteen Two Months later in Uncle John's Basement

The group reassembles, everyone tripping over the mess created building the super computer.

Toni starts up the computer, "Okay everybody, pray."

Nick says, "I think this might work." Touches button, monitor lights up. Clapping all around.

George inquires, "So we can look at the accounts now?"

Nick answers, "We can look, and they won't even know we're looking. So we can take our time and see what these boys have been up to."

George looks. "Now there it is, it's actually around a hundred million apiece to the guys we know and love—Harry Winters, Dick Folded, Harry Paulsin, Jake Demon, Harry Patel, Robbie Rube, Allan Brownstreak, a few European CEOs and Aaron Holdit. I guess the law doesn't apply to the Caymans, which I guess makes sense. The real crooks still have to have a place to hide their money. And the real trillions are in the accounts of noncitizens started at the same time the funds were stolen from the Fed."

Nick asks, "Fake identities?"

George muses, "Sure I guess. That's what I would do in case somehow I got caught; there'd still be money in the fake accounts."

"And this computer can just swipe it and not leave a trace," adds Pat.

Toni chimes in, "That's the idea."

Jeff asks, "Won't these guys miss their money?"

Karma

George answers, "Sure but what're they gonna do? They're not supposed to have it, and the banks won't tell on them 'cuz they want the capital to invest and make more."

Toni is still surprised, "How did this all happen?"

George explains, "Well it all started with Alan Brownstreak, although he had plenty of willing accomplices. Actually, a lot of brilliant people who were employed in Cold War tactics went into finance when the Cold War ended."

Jeff exclaims, "Brilliant!"

George continues to explain, "Brilliant in a sneaky, thieving way. When Brownstreak deregulated banking, it allowed the banks to put financial products—mortgages, pension funds—into a lump sum and sell them to other financial institutions, and everyone involved would get a cut."

George piles the napkins and plasticware to show how these were all lumped together.

Toni observes, "Oh, I see, like a sandwich of financial products."

George agrees, "Right. If that wasn't enough, they would then bet against their investments by making sure they were insured with that big AI something, AIG, and we know what happened with them."

Pat asks, "What happened to them?"

"Went down like a house of cards when they couldn't insure all the bad investments. They said these were complex systems and the average Joe couldn't understand them. So just like in the *Emperor's New Clothes,* the government guys went along; no one wanted to be called stupid," explains George.

Pat continues to ask, "Really, nobody questioned it? How does it work?"

George continues to explain, "I'll just explain the mortgages. It used to be when a bank gave a person a mortgage, the money came from their depositors who fully expected to be paid back. So they were careful who they lent their money to. More recently they sold the mortgages to other financial institutions and got paid a bonus for every mortgage they wrote. So they wrote predatory loans knowing people couldn't pay, sold them off, and got a bonus."

Toni remarks, "That's amazing that they wrote loans knowing people couldn't pay them back."

George comments, "These people also rated bad investments as AAA and got pension funds and even school boards to invest in them."

Toni asks shocked, "How did they present these securitizations as safe?"

George continues, "After they bundled the mortgages, they split them up into tranches. The highest tranche would be rated AAA, which is the rating signifying that it is as safe as a US Treasury bond. The idea was that the first money that came in would go straight to the people that invested in the highest tranche. Once those were all paid, if there was money left, the investors in the next tranche would get paid, and so on."

Pat asks again, "Why is that so bad?"

George again continues to explain, "This method is not really a problem. The shit really hit the fan when they combined the lower tranches and started to then tranche them as well. These are called 'collateralized debt obligations'. So the lowest tranche would get diced up, and the first tranche of the shit mortgages would get a AAA rating, which again is saying that it is as safe as a US Treasury bond. Everyone wanted to get their hands on these so-called safe securities, so the banks kept lending. The bankers got bonuses, and of course these investments went bust. Now people are out of their pension funds, houses were lost, and school boards are short of their funds. In the meantime Wall Street stole, partied, and no one went to jail."

Karma

Toni screams, "They did in Iceland and Ireland!"

George continues, "Alan Brownstreak was warned and warned and warned but refused to do anything about it. He surely belongs in jail as do the rest of them. They knew when they got so big the government would bail them out to avoid global catastrophe. The problem is now they are even bigger and can steal and steal and will be bailed out. And now Mr. Sin himself, Paulsin, is busy fuckin' up the banks in China." Arms now flailing wildly. "Now Mr. Paulsin will be trying to get the Chinese to see the Emperor's new clothes again, and again they say their financial packages are so complex one has to be really smart to understand, and one by one they can see the Emperor's new clothes."

Jeff chimes in, "How come you didn't jump in and get rich with the rest of the thieves?"

George says sheepishly, "I got caught embezzling from a small firm, and then I got into the junk, on and off."

"What'd you like the best?" presses Jeff.

George smiles thinking of it. "Oh, the coke was great, made me feel like a god."

Jeff asks, "How'd you get off it?"

George answers, "Well when you're cuttin' your coke with an AARP card, it's time to quit. Plus you can't get any good coke anymore, anyway."

Jeff presses, "You have an AARP card?"

George says, "Sure, I'm over fifty. Anyway the guys who brought down the world got to keep their money and no jail time."

Pat chimes in, "What a bunch of greedy bastards!"

Whitey pipes up, "Ya, and to think we were the ones locked up. They need to be arrested! You're right, Toni, they need to do here what they did in Iceland and Ireland. Lock up the bastards!"

Nick breaks in, "No, this is better; we're hitting them in the wallet, and there's not a damn thing they can do about it."

George getting back to business, "So I got everybody their fake identities. I know a good counterfeiter that owed me one. Pat, you're a Russian - Vladimir Tolstoy, Whitey, a Swede - Lars Svenson, Jeff, you're a Palestinian businessman - Ibrahim Pasha, Toni - Maria Gonzalez from Me-hi-co, and lastly Nick—"

Nick cuts him off, "Oh, I'm not taking any."

George cries, "Are you crazy? What are you gonna do?"

Nick explains, "I'm still gonna work. They may suspect me, but they'll know it's me if I go on the lam. I'm just gonna keep going to work every day. Especially since I'll likely be in charge of the place since Alan's gone."

George insists, "But still, don't you want a million now?"

Nick says, "It'd be nice, but..."

Toni speaks up, "Well, I'm taking my million, especially since they can't trace it. Okay, we'll just put it in the Cayman's for ourselves, but the bulk of the six trillion is put back into the ninety-nine percenters' bank accounts."

Nick says, "Yeah, okay it's all programmed in."

Toni explains, "There's roughly one hundred million bank accounts; sadly, ninety million have less than fifty thousand dollars. This is where we're going to be transferring the bulk of the money—back to the people. This divided by six trillion equals about four and a half trillion, then one and a half trillion goes back to the Fed."

Karma

Pat asks, "What are the people going to think about that new money in their account?"

Toni explains, "I'm sending a message to each that this is a present from 'Robin Hood'. A onetime present and guard your money."

Pat shrieks, "Cool!"

George says, "It will just transfer in a few seconds, maybe milliseconds."

Toni cries, "Yeah, if it works. Everybody pray!"

George holds his l'chaim medal, Jeff folds his hands and bows head. Pat and Nick look upward and say a prayer.

Toni prays softly, "Oh please, Señora de la Guadalupe, please ask your Son to help us." Looking closely, Our Lady is reflected upside down in her irises. She presses a button. *Zing*, noise, lights falter, then go out.

Pat asks, "Did it work?"

Toni replies, "I think so, I hope so, I felt like La Señora answered."

George suggests, "So we can't look and see?"

Toni answers, "Not on this computer; it's fried now."

Nick suggests, "But we can check on a P.C. if the money got transferred into your personal accounts with the fake IDs."

They trip again over each other on the way to the other P.C. George puts in info, and an account with one million in his fake ID pops up. Checks for Whitey, Jeff, Pat, and Toni.

Pat says shocked, "I can't believe it. I may start goin' to church again."

Jeff asks, "And they'll never trace it? Never find us? Never break our legs?"

Nick assuredly, "NO, no, and definitely no. If they find you, I'm sure they'd do more than break your legs."

George says, "I hate saying 'they' but we really don't know who 'they' are except that they're very powerful to pull this one off."

Nick comments, "Well, they had inside help boys. So what do you say we send that old Ben BerNasty a little note?"

Pat interrupts, "First, time to celebrate, bro."

Nick looking at Toni.

Nick says, "Later, we have our own private celebration to tend to." All smile knowingly.

Toni smiles, "Let's get to it."

Karma

Chapter Twenty Toni's House

Toni and Nick are walking through Toni's hallway on the way to her bedroom. Toni looking at the statue of the Blessed Mother.

Toni says, "Gracias, mi Madre."

Nick asks, "What?"

Toni answers, "Nothing."

In the bedroom, Toni wraps her arms around Nick. Toni moans, "Hold me, I've waited so long!"

Nick holding Toni's face in his hands, "Is this real? Is this really happening? I feel like I just woke up from a fifteen-year nightmare and finally got my life back."

Toni whispers, "I'm real, all right."

They start kissing and taking off clothes, eventually ending up in bed. Finally in bed, afterward.

Nick moans, "Oh my God!"

Toni exclaims, "Are you kidding me?"

Nick says excitedly, "I feel like I've just been reborn!"

Toni replies, "Well, we're together now and nothing can keep us apart."

Nick agrees, "True soul mates."

Karma

Chapter Twenty-One Inside the Whitehouse

Ben BerNasty is opening an email. The message reads, "We know you're a high-ranking official on the board for the Federal Reserve, but this is OUR money and don't steal it again! We've put some of the money back in the Federal Reserve and a lot of it back into the multitudes' bank accounts. We're watching you!" The message then disintegrates.

Ben is perspiring nervously and looks over his shoulder. He thinks this is probably a dream.

Somewhere the tune "I Say a Little Prayer for You" is playing.

Karma

Chapter Twenty-Two A Very Nice Ending

Woman looks lovingly at George, and he smiles as they enter the synagogue.

Jeff with girl from the 7-Eleven are going into a mosque.

Pat is in front of a mirror putting on a tie, then has two girls on his arms, ready to party.

Toni and Nick are going into a church hand in hand. Joan, Nick's mother is in the pew and for whatever reason turns around and sees them walking in. Her eyes go wide, and she nudges the woman in the pew next to her. In a whisper she says, "Look, look, Nick is in church with that beautiful girl he's seeing that I told you about. They'll have beautiful children, don't you think?"

Woman in pew says, "Don't go countin' your grandchildren before they're hatched."

Joan looks confused, "What?"

Woman in pew says, "You know what I mean."

Karma

Chapter Twenty-Three Nick and Toni's Future

At Nick's work, everyone is clapping as he announces he is the new boss. He then introduces Toni and says he's hired her for anti cyber terrorism.

Six months later, Toni and Nick are in front of the University of Illinois. They are there to attend a banking seminar. Harry Paulsin, now an instructor there, is heading to the seminar. He spots Nick and Toni and approaches them.

Harry starts out, "So Nick, you the big man now that Alan is gone? Who's the pretty girl?"

Nick says dryly, "She's a new hire. She can track down any hacker and any funny business going on, like money disappearing from the Federal Reserve." Now Toni and Harry are shaking hands.

Toni says, "Very nice to meet you."

"Likewise," Harry murmurs.

They walk away, and Harry dials a number into his cell phone. Harry speaks in a low voice into his phone, "I think I know who took the money!"

Picture of the seven Regan Sisters

Mary Boyle

Margaret Regan